THIS

BOOK

BELONGS

TO_____

DISNEY'S
SMALL WORLD LIBRARY

DONALD JOINS THE MOUNTIES
An Adventure in Canada

GROLIER ENTERPRISES INC.
DANBURY, CONNECTICUT

© The Walt Disney Company. All rights reserved.
Printed in the United States of America.
Developed by The Walt Disney Company in conjunction with Nancy Hall, Inc.
ISBN: 0-7172-8220-1

Donald Duck stepped off the train at Toronto's Union
Station. This was the moment he had been waiting for.
Ever since he had read about the Royal Canadian
Mounted Police, all he could think about was becoming a
Mountie. Now he was in Canada at last!

Donald's cousin, George LeDuck, was at the station to greet him. "Welcome!" he cried. "I can't wait to show you around. Canada is a very big country, and I want you to see everything!"

"Where can we find some Mounties?" called Donald, but George was already too far ahead of him to hear.

"This is the tallest tower in the world," said George, pointing to the famous CN Tower. "Just wait until you see the view from the top!"

"How do we get up there?" asked Donald.

"If you'd like, we can take the elevator," said George. "I myself prefer to walk up the stairs. It makes you realize how tall this tower really is. But if you're too tired . . ."

"Of course I'm not too tired," interrupted Donald. "Mounties never get tired," he said to himself.

When they reached the top, George led Donald over to a window.

"Look at this view!" exclaimed George. "Isn't it beautiful?"

Donald couldn't answer. He was out of breath!

Donald and George ate lunch at the revolving restaurant at the top of the tower. Donald tried to tell George about his plans to become a Mountie, but George had other things on his mind.

"Let's talk about the Mounties later, Donald," said George. "Right now we have more sightseeing to do."

They headed over to Exhibition Park, where the Canadian National Exhibition was taking place.

"There's so much to see here!" said George enthusiastically. "Horse shows, dog shows, flower shows—and look at this wonderful science fair."

Donald had to jog just to keep up with George. "Are there any furniture exhibits?" he asked. "Maybe someone has a nice, comfortable bed I could try out!"

After Exhibition Park, George and Donald went to a huge building in the middle of the city.

"This is Casa Loma," said George. "It's the largest castle in North America. Let's go on a tour—but please be sure to stay with the group. With 98 rooms, it's easy to get lost."

"Mounties never get lost," thought Donald. "I'm sure it would be all right if I did some exploring on my own," he said to himself, sneaking away from the tour.

Soon Donald realized he didn't know where he was.
He leaned against a wall to rest. Suddenly, the wall
swung around and Donald found himself in a long tunnel.
He walked to the end of it and found the fanciest stable
he had ever seen! It had marble walls and even the water
troughs were made of porcelain.

Just then the guide appeared beside him.

"There you are!" she said, laughing. "Someone gets
lost on every tour, and I always know to look in this secret
passage."

When George and Donald left the castle, they saw a parade coming down the street.

"Look!" cried Donald. "It's the Royal Canadian Mounted Police!"

"We Canadians think they are the finest police force in the world," said George proudly.

"I like their uniforms, too. Don't you think I would look great in one?" Donald asked. Before George could answer, Donald called to the Mountie who was closest to him. "Hey! Where do I sign up to be a Mountie?"

"You'd have to go to the Mountie headquarters over there," the Mountie replied, pointing to a nearby building. "But I don't think you . . ."

Donald didn't wait to hear the rest of what the Mountie had to say. He was already on his way.

Donald burst through the doors of the Mountie headquarters. "Where do I apply?" he asked breathlessly. The sergeant sitting behind the desk gave Donald a form. Donald quickly filled it in and handed it back.

"I'm sorry," the sergeant told Donald after reading the application. "In order to be a Mountie you must be a Canadian citizen."

Donald walked out of the headquarters feeling sad. He knew he would make a great Mountie. But he'd have to figure out a way to prove it.

Suddenly he had an idea. "I've got it!" he cried. "I'll practice being a Mountie and doing good deeds. Once the Mounties see what a fine job I'm doing, they'll hire me right away—even though I'm not a Canadian citizen."

That night Donald asked George for his advice. George suggested that the Algonquin Provincial Park would be a good place to practice.

The very next day Donald boarded the train for the park. George handed him a present.

Donald unwrapped the package. "A History of the Royal Canadian Mounted Police!" he said. "Thanks!"

Donald waved good-bye to George as the train began to move. The train took him past beautiful green forests, rocky canyons, and sparkling lakes, but Donald was too busy with his book to take notice of the scenery.

Donald got off the train near the park. There he saw a group of people heading for a bus. They were going on a tour of an old mine.

"Here's my chance," thought Donald. "Abandoned mines can be very dangerous. These people may need my help!"

Donald hopped on the bus and followed the group to the mine.

Inside the mine, Donald heard a woman call to her husband.

"Oh, Harold!" the woman said. "Look at this beautiful stone I found on the ground!"

Donald watched as the woman put the sparkling gem in her pocket.

Donald raced out of the mine and ran to the nearest
Mountie post to report the crime.

"Thanks for trying to help," said one of the Mounties.
"But this is a special event called the Gemboree,"
he explained. "During this time tourists are allowed to
keep any stones and minerals they find."

Donald sheepishly left the Mountie post and returned to the park.

"I'll have to be more careful about what I report," he thought with determination.

Soon Donald came upon a clearing where all of the trees had been chopped down. He raced off to find a Mountie.

"Those trees were cut down by beavers," explained the Mountie. "They use the trees to build dams and make their homes."

"I made another big mistake!" thought Donald. He continued on his way, but it wasn't long before he heard a disturbing sound. Donald peeked through the trees.

"They aren't beavers!" cried Donald. "Those people are using a chain saw to cut down the trees!"

Donald ran back to find the Mountie.

"I saw people cutting down trees this time!" cried Donald. "And I don't think they need them to build dams."

"Of course not," said the Mountie, laughing. "Those people are loggers. Logging is allowed in the park during the summer months."

"I guess I'm not familiar with all the rules around here," muttered Donald.

Donald was very tired from all his hiking, so he decided to set up camp for the night. He tried to go to sleep, but the forest noises kept him awake.

"Whooo, whooooo," called an animal. "That's only an owl," Donald said, comforting himself.

Then Donald heard a sound he couldn't ignore.

"Wolves!" he cried, as the howls got louder and louder.

Donald ran to get help.

"Wolves!" he shouted when he found a Mountie. "I've never heard such howling. Something terrible must be happening!"

"Take it easy," said the Mountie, chuckling. "Nothing terrible is going on. This park happens to have the only packs of timber wolves in the world."

"Timber wolves like to howl together," the Mountie continued. "Every year at this time, people come to the park to sing along with the wolves. That's why the howling is so loud tonight."

"Oh," said Donald, feeling silly. "I didn't know."

He returned to his sleeping bag, but he refused to be discouraged. "All I need is a good night's rest," he said to himself. "Tomorrow is another day."

The next day Donald explored a different part of the park.

"Sooner or later I'll do something really helpful," he thought. "Then the Mounties will hire me!"

Just then Donald saw some interesting-looking rocks. When he got closer, however, he saw that they were covered with drawings.

"Graffiti!" he cried. "I'd better report this right away!"

Donald found a Mountie and led him to the site.

"Isn't this terrible?" Donald said, pointing to the rocks. "People are drawing all over park property. We've got to catch these vandals!"

"That would be very difficult," the Mountie said. "These drawings were done by the Algonquin Indians over five hundred years ago. Thanks anyway, though, for trying to help."

Donald tried to keep himself from getting discouraged. He continued on his way, ready to act at the first sign of trouble. Then he took a deep breath.

There was the faintest trace of smoke in the air. Donald looked off into the distance and saw smoke rising above the trees.

"Fires are illegal here in dry weather," he said, racing to report the fire. "That's one thing I'm sure of!"

The Mountie pulled Donald up onto his horse. "I'll bet that's the group of missing campers!" said the Mountie. "Show me where you saw the smoke!"

It wasn't long before they found the group of campers around a fire.

"Boy, are we glad to see you," said one of them. "We've been lost for days."

"You have Donald to thank," said the Mountie.

Donald smiled proudly.

A few days later the Mounties held a ceremony for Donald in the International Peace Garden. All the campers were there and so was cousin George.

The sergeant stepped up to the podium. "For your heroic rescue of the campers," he said, "and for all the hard work you've done, we hereby make you an honorary member of the Royal Canadian Mounted Police." The sergeant presented Donald with a Maple Leaf pin.

"This is the proudest day of my life!" said Donald.

"I never thought you'd get to be a Mountie," admitted George. "But you really did it. You had a dream and you didn't give up."

"Mounties never give up," beamed Donald. "Everyone knows that!"

Did You Know...?

There are many different customs and places that make each country special. Do you remember some of the things below from the story?

Toronto is Canada's largest city. It has some of the country's most interesting buildings. City Hall is made up of two curved buildings with a building between them that is shaped like a flying saucer.

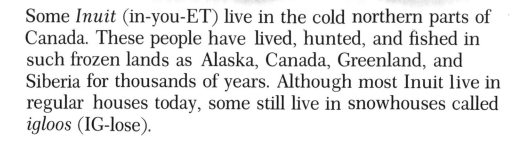

Some *Inuit* (in-you-ET) live in the cold northern parts of Canada. These people have lived, hunted, and fished in such frozen lands as Alaska, Canada, Greenland, and Siberia for thousands of years. Although most Inuit live in regular houses today, some still live in snowhouses called *igloos* (IG-lose).

The Royal Canadian Mounted Police, better known as the "Mounties," was formed in 1873. The Mounties' original job was to enforce the law in Canada's wild West. Mounties, who once rode on horseback, today travel by car, motorcycle, airplane, and even snowmobile to enforce law in all parts of Canada.

The International Peace Garden lies on the Canadian-United States border. It is a symbol of friendship between the two countries. Besides beautiful flowers, the Peace Garden contains nature trails, campgrounds, a chapel, and a summer music camp.

The saying "busy as a beaver" is a true one. Beavers use their strong teeth to cut down trees around ponds. They eat the bark of the trees, and some beavers use the wood to build two-level homes in ponds. Canadians admire the hard-working beaver and consider it one of their national symbols.

Canada's timber wolves hunt in packs. Each pack guards its own large hunting territory very carefully.

Forestry is important in Canada. Trees are cut down by
loggers, hauled to rivers, and then floated or carried in
barges to mills. Here the logs are turned into lumber,
pulp, paper, and other products.

Ontario's Algonquin Provincial Park
is one of Canada's most popular
wilderness areas. It is named after
the Algonquin Indians, one of the
Native American tribes that lived
in Canada before European
settlers came. Canadians from
all over come to the park to
hike, camp, and fish.